# Navigate your Cosmos

# TABLE OF CONTENTS

☼ ☼ ☼

# acknowledgement

I want to begin by expressing my heartfelt gratitude to my family, and especially to my mother, who has been a constant source of inspiration and support in shaping me into the person I am today. It was her encouragement that first sparked my interest in researching the circadian rhythm and ultimately led me to create this book. I cannot thank you enough, and I truly believe you deserve half the credit for every accomplishment I've achieved. To all of my mentors, thank you for your unwavering support throughout this entire journey—from the early stages of research and brainstorming to the final steps of bringing my book to life. Your guidance, encouragement, and belief in me have been invaluable, and I am deeply grateful for everything you've done to help me learn, grow, and reach new heights.

Imagine if I told you there's a hidden clock inside your body, ticking away, guiding everything from when you feel energized to when you start craving sleep. It's called the circadian rhythm, and it's been around since the time of our ancestors. But here's the twist: most of us are totally out of sync with it. Ever felt groggy in the morning, even after a long night's sleep? Or strangely awake at midnight on a school night? That's your circadian rhythm giving you a nudge, saying, 'Hey, something's off!' In this book, we're going to explore how understanding this inner clock can boost your focus, improve your mood, and even change how you feel every day.

# The Clock inside you

The world around us is constantly changing, with day turning to night and seasons shifting, but what keeps us in sync with these changes? The answer lies in our circadian rhythm—a biological clock that regulates our sleep-wake cycles, energy levels, and various body functions. Understanding this rhythm is the first step toward improving our overall health and well-being.

Your body's internal clock—known as the circadian rhythm—keeps time like an unseen, steady beat, orchestrating the ebb and flow of countless processes. It's the reason you feel awake in the morning and sleepy at night. This rhythm governs not just when you sleep, but also when you eat, when you're alert, and when you're ready to rest. While we may think of time in hours and minutes, your body measures it in the form of the circadian rhythm, a 24-hour internal cycle influenced by light and darkness.

The circadian rhythm is essentially a 24-hour cycle that affects many of your bodily functions. It's primarily synchronized by light exposure, which signals the brain to release specific hormones that tell your body whether it's time to be awake or asleep. The most significant external cue for regulating this rhythm is light—more specifically, the transition from light to dark. During the day, exposure to natural light signals your body to be awake and alert, while as darkness falls, your body begins preparing for rest.

However, circadian rhythms are more than just your sleep-wake cycle. They affect a wide range of processes, from hormone production and digestion to brain function and mood regulation.

This rhythm aligns with the natural cycle of the Earth, but is influenced by external factors such as light, temperature, and activities.

For real-life examples of Circadian Rhythm in action, Consider the experience of jet lag—a common occurrence for travelers crossing multiple time zones. When you travel east or west, your circadian rhythm struggles to adapt to the new local time, leading to fatigue, difficulty sleeping, and irritability. The body's internal clock is out of sync with the external environment, causing disruption in your sleep-wake patterns until your rhythm realigns with the new time zone.

Shift workers, too, often struggle with misalignment of their circadian rhythm. Those working night shifts or rotating schedules frequently find themselves fighting against their natural sleep-wake cycle, leading to sleep deprivation, poor quality sleep, and even higher risks for conditions like heart disease and obesity. Their bodies are forced to sleep during the day when the circadian rhythm signals the body to stay awake, disrupting not only sleep but also hormone regulation and overall health.

Why is this internal clock so important? When your circadian rhythm operates smoothly, it contributes to one's overall health. From optimizing sleep to regulating metabolism, your circadian rhythm helps ensure that everything happens at the right time. For example, it influences hormone levels, body temperature, and even the regulation of important metabolic processes like digestion and blood sugar regulation.

When the rhythm is disrupted, the consequences can be far-reaching. Misalignment of the circadian rhythm can lead to sleep disorders, depression, and chronic conditions like obesity and heart disease. It governs how your body handles stress, mood swings, and energy levels throughout the day. Without the proper alignment, the body's ability to regulate these processes effectively can be severely hindered and can have profound impact on various aspects of your day-to-day life such as,

# Circadian Rythm Clock

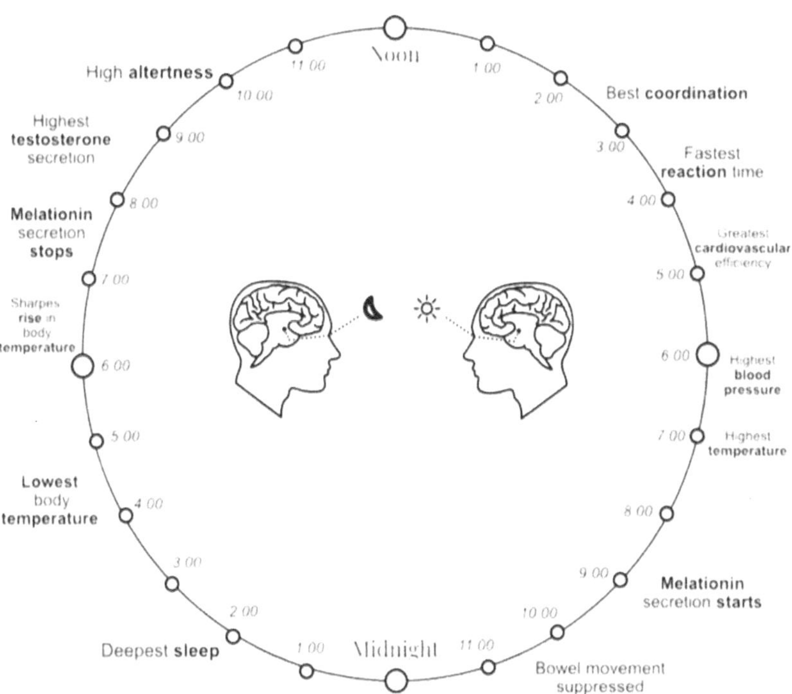

**Energy Levels:** Your circadian rhythm plays a large role in regulating when you feel most energetic. For many people, the body experiences a peak in energy in the morning and a natural dip in the afternoon. By understanding this rhythm, you can structure your day around these natural fluctuations to optimize productivity.

**Mental Alertness:** Your brain's ability to focus and stay alert follows a predictable pattern, influenced by the circadian rhythm. Cognitive performance tends to be sharper in the morning when cortisol levels are high. Later in the day, mental clarity often diminishes as the body prepares for rest, explaining the afternoon slump many people experience.

**Mood Regulation:** The circadian rhythm also influences your emotional state. Disruptions in this rhythm can lead to irritability, anxiety, and even more serious conditions like depression. Aligning your circadian rhythm with natural day-night cycles can help improve overall mood and mental well-being.

**Sleep Quality:** Of course, one of the primary functions of the circadian rhythm is regulating sleep. The timing of your sleep—when you go to bed and when you wake up—determines the quality and length of your sleep, which directly impacts overall health and well-being.

Understanding the circadian rhythm is not just important for scientists or medical professionals—it's something that can benefit everyone. By aligning your schedule with the natural rhythms of your body, you can enhance your overall health, increase productivity, and improve your emotional well-being. Whether you're a teenager struggling with sleep issues, an adult dealing with stress, or someone simply looking for more energy throughout the day, understanding the science behind your internal clock is the key.

# How the rhythm works

Every day, as the sun rises and sets, your body synchronizes with the natural world around it. This isn't just a coincidence; it's the work of a remarkable internal mechanism that has been fine-tuned over millions of years, your circadian rhythm. The process that governs this rhythm is controlled by a tiny, but incredibly powerful, cluster of cells deep in your brain—known as the **suprachiasmatic nucleus (SCN)**. The SCN is the heart of your body's internal clock, a network of about 20,000 nerve cells nestled in the hypothalamus, just above the point where your optic nerves cross. Although the SCN is smaller than a grain of rice, its influence is enormous. It tells your body when to wake up, when to sleep, when to eat, and when to perform essential functions like digesting food or repairing tissues. Essentially, it acts as the conductor of a grand biological orchestra, coordinating the rhythm of nearly every cell, organ, and system in your body. The SCN is constantly in sync with the light-dark cycle of the world around you. Light, particularly sunlight, acts as the most powerful signal to reset this internal clock. When sunlight hits specialized cells in your retina, it sends a signal directly to the SCN, helping to synchronize your body's internal rhythm with the external environment. This process is incredibly precise. The SCN makes sure that your body is fully awake and alert during the day when you need energy, and that it relaxes and prepares for rest when it's time to sleep. Now, Let's understand this concept in depth with solid scientific reasoning. When sunlight enters the eyes, it activates specialized retinal cells known as intrinsically photosensitive retinal ganglion cells (ipRGCs), which send direct signals to the suprachiasmatic nucleus (SCN) in the hypothalamus.

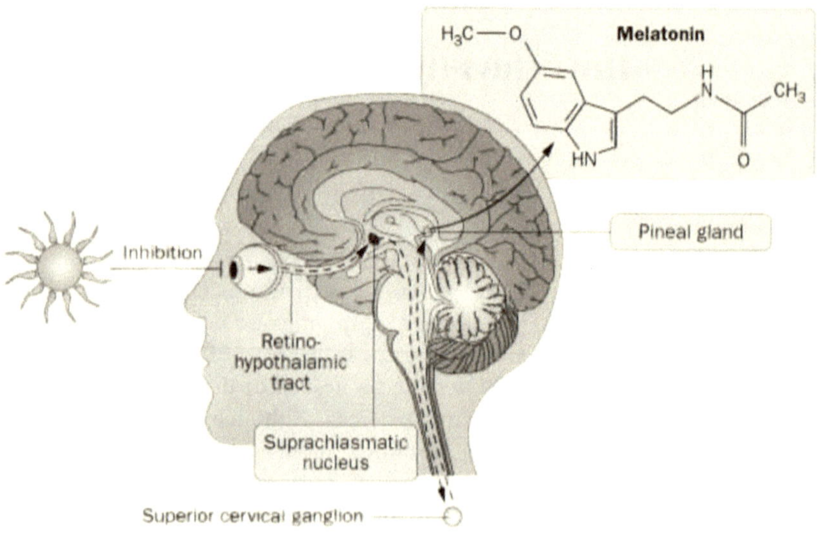


H₃C—O
Melatonin
H
N
CH₃
O
HN
Inhibition
Retino-
hypothalamic
tract
Suprachiasmatic
nucleus
Superior cervical ganglion
Pineal gland

This signal is what resets the body's internal clock each day, ensuring that it aligns with the natural light-dark cycle. The relationship between light and the circadian rhythm is finely tuned, and its timing is crucial.

Bright light exposure, especially in the morning, plays an essential role in signaling the body to wake up and start the day. This morning light increases cortisol levels, boosting alertness and setting the tone for the day's activities. Additionally, light exposure during the day supports cognitive performance and energy levels. But light isn't only about its intensity; its wavelength also matters. Blue light, emitted by both the sun and artificial sources such as smartphones, tablets, and LED lights, has a particularly strong influence on the circadian rhythm. During the day, blue light helps keep the internal clock synchronized. However, in the evening, it becomes problematic. Blue light exposure late at night, particularly from screens, delays melatonin production—the hormone responsible for initiating sleep. This delay disrupts the sleep-wake cycle, making it more difficult to fall asleep at the proper time. Research from Harvard Medical School has shown that just two hours of exposure to blue light before bedtime can delay melatonin release by up to 23%, pushing back sleep onset by as much as 90 minutes. This delay affects not only the timing of sleep but also its quality, resulting in shorter, less restorative sleep. Poor sleep can then disrupt hormonal regulation, cognitive function, and emotional balance. It's not just the blue light emitted by screens that interferes with the circadian rhythm. The pervasive use of artificial lighting, particularly in urban environments, keeps people exposed to light far longer than intended. Even dim light can affect the SCN and prevent the body from properly winding down at night. While light is critical for daytime alertness, exposure to artificial light after sunset sends mixed signals to the body, confusing its internal clock. When the circadian rhythm is disrupted by improper light exposure, the consequences are far-reaching. Here are some of the most common effects:

**Sleep Disruption**: The suppression of melatonin caused by blue light exposure leads to difficulty falling asleep, resulting in sleep deprivation and lower sleep quality.

**Reduced Sleep Duration**: A delayed sleep onset reduces the overall amount of sleep, limiting the body's ability to undergo crucial sleep cycles needed for physical and cognitive recovery.

**Mood Disorders**: Irregular light exposure and poor sleep can contribute to mood disorders such as anxiety, depression, and irritability. This is because the lack of sleep interferes with the regulation of stress hormones, affecting emotional stability and resilience.

Light is essential for regulating the body's internal clock, but it's not just the amount of light we receive—it's also the timing and type of exposure that truly matter. Morning sunlight, especially within the first hour of waking, acts as a natural cue to reset the circadian rhythm, promoting alertness and energy throughout the day. In contrast, exposure to artificial light, particularly blue light in the evening, disrupts this delicate balance by delaying melatonin production and interfering with sleep quality. By understanding how both light and hormones work together to maintain a healthy circadian rhythm, we can better align our light exposure with our natural biological cycles, optimizing sleep and overall well-being. As much as evening light disrupts the rhythm, morning light is essential in reinforcing it. Exposure to natural light in the morning, especially within the first hour after waking, helps set the circadian clock for the day. This boost of light tells your brain that it's time to be awake, allowing your system to transition smoothly into an alert, active state. This is why morning routines often emphasize getting outside or seeking natural sunlight as soon as possible. It serves as a natural cue to reset the body's rhythm, making it easier to stay alert during the day and prepare for rest at night. For many, even brief exposure to sunlight—around 20 minutes—can significantly improve their circadian rhythm. This is a simple yet effective way to align your internal clock with nature and maintain a more consistent sleep-wake cycle. Without it, the risk of misalignment increases, which may contribute to sleep disorders, low energy, and diminished cognitive performance. Within the circadian rhythm, hormones are the unseen conductors guiding the symphony of our daily cycles. These chemical messengers not only keep time but regulate critical processes like sleep, alertness, digestion, and even mood. When the rhythm is thrown off balance, these hormones struggle to maintain their melody, leading to a cascade of effects on our body and mind. Cortisol, often known as the "stress hormone," plays a pivotal role in waking us up and preparing us for the day. Under normal circumstances, cortisol levels peak early in the morning, shortly after we wake up. This surge helps to increase our blood sugar levels, boost our energy, and sharpen our focus. It's the body's natural alarm clock—ensuring that you are alert and ready for action when the day begins. However, when the circadian rhythm is disrupted, cortisol secretion can be misaligned. Late-night screen exposure and irregular sleep patterns lead to delayed cortisol production the next morning, causing grogginess, fatigue, and difficulty focusing. This misalignment, especially when it happens repeatedly, can worsen over time, leaving you in a cycle of constant exhaustion and mental fog. When the day transitions into night, our bodies start preparing for rest. This process is largely controlled by melatonin, the "sleep hormone." Melatonin production ramps up as the environment darkens, signaling to your brain that it's time to wind down and prepare for sleep.

Under typical circumstances, melatonin levels rise around sunset, encouraging deep, restful sleep during the night. But artificial light, especially blue light from phones, laptops, and TVs, can disrupt this process. Blue light mimics daylight, tricking your brain into thinking it's still daytime. As a result, melatonin production is delayed or suppressed, making it harder to fall asleep even when you're physically tired. This is a key reason why late-night screen time is so detrimental to your sleep quality and overall circadian rhythm. While cortisol and melatonin are the most well-known hormones involved in regulating the circadian rhythm, several others also play significant roles like the **Growth Hormone (GH)**: Released during deep sleep, growth hormone helps with tissue repair, muscle building, and immune function. When the circadian rhythm is disrupted, the timing of growth hormone release can be affected, leading to poor recovery, weakened immune function, and muscle fatigue & **Insulin**: This hormone is critical in regulating blood sugar levels and metabolism. The timing of meals significantly impacts insulin sensitivity, as well as the release of insulin. Irregular eating schedules—such as late-night snacking—can cause insulin to be released at odd times, impairing its effectiveness and potentially leading to metabolic issues like insulin resistance and weight gain over time. When these hormones no longer function in harmony, the impact can be widespread. Cognitive function begins to suffer as melatonin and cortisol levels fluctuate. You may notice it's harder to concentrate, retain information, or stay awake during the day. Mood swings become more common, as serotonin production, influenced by circadian rhythms, is thrown out of balance. People often experience anxiety, irritability, or even depression when their internal clocks are misaligned. The disruptions caused by poor sleep, inconsistent eating habits, and light exposure have the potential to affect virtually every system in the body, leading to both short-term consequences like fatigue and stress, as well as long-term health risks, such as diabetes, cardiovascular disease, and obesity. The impact of misaligned hormones goes beyond just feeling tired or sluggish. When hormones like cortisol and melatonin are out of sync, the body's internal systems struggle to maintain balance. This can trigger a domino effect across several aspects of mental and physical health like,

Cognitive Decline: Reduced cognitive function makes learning and memory more difficult. In academic settings, students may struggle to concentrate, leading to poor performance.

Weakened Immune System: Chronic disruption of circadian rhythms weakens the immune system, making you more susceptible to illnesses and infections.

Metabolic Issues: Irregular eating habits, combined with disrupted insulin and growth hormone cycles, can contribute to metabolic disorders, including obesity, type 2 diabetes, and heart disease.

Sleep, that essential yet often overlooked cornerstone of health, is intricately tied to the circadian rhythm. It's not just a passive activity but a highly active process that restores our bodies and minds. The quality of our sleep, and the timing of it, is crucial for our overall well-being. When our circadian rhythm is in sync, sleep becomes an incredibly restorative experience, but when disrupted, the results can be devastating, affecting everything from memory to immune function.

Sleep is a complex process involving several stages, all of which play unique roles in rejuvenating the body and mind. These stages are divided into Non-Rapid Eye Movement (NREM) and Rapid Eye Movement (REM) sleep, with each phase serving a specific purpose. NREM Sleep: This is the restorative sleep that helps your body recover from the wear and tear of the day. It's during this phase that growth hormone is released, aiding in tissue repair, muscle growth, and immune function. NREM sleep is also critical for memory consolidation—essential for learning and cognitive function. It's made up of three stages: light sleep, deep sleep, and the very deep restorative sleep known as slow-wave sleep (SWS). REM Sleep: REM sleep is the stage where vivid dreams occur. During this phase, the brain becomes highly active, almost like it's awake, while the body remains paralyzed to prevent us from physically acting out our dreams. REM sleep is essential for emotional regulation, problem-solving, and processing memories. It's a time when the brain sorts and stores information from the day, allowing us to think more clearly the following day. The body's circadian rhythm regulates the transitions between these sleep stages, ensuring that you cycle through them appropriately. However, disturbances in your internal clock—due to irregular sleep times, light exposure at night, or stress—can hinder your ability to reach the deeper stages of sleep, diminishing its restorative benefits. Timing is crucial for sleep, and the circadian rhythm plays a major role in regulating when we feel sleepy and when we feel alert. Our natural sleep-wake cycle is typically about 24 hours, synchronized with the day-night cycle. The hormone melatonin, secreted in response to darkness, promotes sleepiness as night falls, while light inhibits melatonin production, helping us wake up. When sleep occurs in alignment with your circadian rhythm, you fall asleep easily and experience deep, restful sleep. However, if you stay up too late or wake up at irregular times, the timing of melatonin release becomes disrupted. This misalignment can make it harder to fall asleep and disrupt your entire sleep cycle, leading to poorer sleep quality and shorter sleep duration. Inadequate sleep affects both cognitive performance and physical health. Memory retention, concentration, and decision-making abilities suffer as your brain misses out on the deep sleep necessary for memory consolidation. The body also struggles to repair itself, leading to increased inflammation, a weakened immune system, and an increased risk for diseases like diabetes and heart disease.

When the circadian rhythm is disrupted—whether by travel, shift work, or inconsistent sleep habits—the effects of sleep deprivation become stark. Research shows that lack of sleep is linked to a wide range of health problems:

Cognitive Impairment: Sleep deprivation hampers attention, memory, and learning. A study by the National Sleep Foundation found that individuals who slept less than six hours a night performed significantly worse on memory recall tasks and had a slower reaction time than those who got a full 7-9 hours of sleep.

Emotional Instability: Chronic sleep deprivation leads to increased irritability, anxiety, and mood swings. In fact, a Harvard Medical School study on sleep deprivation found that individuals who received less than five hours of sleep were significantly more likely to report feelings of sadness, stress, and hopelessness compared to those who slept more.

Immune System Suppression: Sleep is a critical period for immune system functioning. During deep sleep, the body produces proteins that strengthen the immune system and combat infection. A study from the University of California, San Francisco showed that participants who slept for less than six hours per night were 4.5 times more likely to catch a cold than those who slept eight hours or more.

Increased Risk for Chronic Diseases: Ongoing sleep deprivation has been linked to long-term health issues such as obesity, diabetes, heart disease, and hypertension. A Harvard study found that people who sleep fewer than 6 hours a night have a significantly higher risk of developing cardiovascular disease due to increased inflammation and disrupted metabolic processes.

For those with poor sleep habits or individuals working irregular hours, there exists a vicious cycle: disruption of the circadian rhythm leads to poor sleep quality, which in turn exacerbates the symptoms of sleep deprivation. The effects of poor sleep compound over time, creating a feedback loop of increasing fatigue, irritability, and difficulty in maintaining regular sleep patterns. For example, shift workers, who often sleep during the day and work at night, face the constant challenge of trying to adjust their circadian rhythms to a schedule that is out of sync with natural light patterns. This misalignment not only results in insufficient sleep but also disrupts the natural sleep-wake cycle, leading to chronic sleep deprivation, decreased cognitive function, and an increased risk of health problems.

In our fast-paced world, the rhythm of life is often out of sync with the natural rhythm of our bodies. Our choices, from the way we sleep to how we eat and manage stress, can quietly disrupt the delicate balance of our circadian rhythm. These lifestyle factors, though often overlooked, hold immense power over our well-being. Let's delve into how each of these elements plays a part in shaping our internal clocks. One of the most pervasive disruptions to the circadian rhythm is irregular sleep. The familiar experience of staying up late over the weekend and struggling to return to a normal schedule the following week isn't just a mild inconvenience; it's a disruption that reverberates through your body's internal clock. This phenomenon, often called 'social jetlag,' occurs when we shift our sleep time by hours, throwing off the body's natural rhythm. Even seemingly minor shifts in sleep timing can have cascading effects, extending far beyond grogginess. A 2020 study in The Journal of Neuroscience uncovered how irregular sleep timing impairs memory retention, cognitive performance, and decision-making. People who frequently stay up late or alter their sleep schedules can experience slower reaction times and foggy thinking—symptoms that linger long after waking. But the effects don't stop with the brain. Irregular sleep patterns also interfere with metabolic processes, especially insulin sensitivity. This disruption can make it harder for your body to regulate blood sugar and process food effectively, increasing the risk of weight gain, diabetes, and other metabolic conditions. In today's digital age, blue light has become an insidious disruptor of our circadian rhythm. Phones, laptops, and even energy-efficient light bulbs emit this artificial blue light, which tricks the brain into thinking it's still daytime. As a result, melatonin—the hormone responsible for signaling that it's time to sleep—is delayed. In a pivotal 2011 study by Harvard Medical School, researchers found that exposure to blue light before bed could delay melatonin production by up to three hours. This delay impacts both the timing and quality of sleep. When melatonin levels remain low, it becomes harder to fall asleep and stay asleep, leading to poorer rest and a misaligned internal clock. Stress is another major factor that can wreak havoc on your circadian rhythm. Cortisol, the hormone responsible for managing the body's stress response, follows its own rhythm—rising in the morning to wake you up and gradually decreasing throughout the day. However, when stress becomes chronic, it disrupts the natural rhythm of cortisol, particularly in the evening. Elevated cortisol levels at night can prevent the body from relaxing and falling asleep. A study published in The Journal of Clinical Endocrinology and Metabolism in 2013 found that people with elevated cortisol levels at night had significantly worse sleep quality and a misaligned circadian rhythm. Chronic stress not only elevates cortisol but also ramps up adrenaline and other stress hormones, keeping the body on high alert when it should be winding down for rest.

What and when you eat are crucial to maintaining a balanced circadian rhythm. The body's internal clocks extend beyond the brain to other organs, including the digestive system. This means that meal timing—particularly late-night eating—can disrupt the synchronization of your body's clocks. A study from the International Journal of Obesity found that people who ate late at night experienced increased insulin resistance and quicker weight gain compared to those who ate earlier. This happens because the body's metabolism is optimized for daytime activity. When food is consumed late, the digestive system is forced to work harder when it should be winding down for rest.
Food choices also play a role in circadian health. Caffeine and sugar, which stimulate the central nervous system, can disrupt sleep and keep you awake longer. On the other hand, foods rich in tryptophan—such as turkey, nuts, and seeds—can help promote the production of melatonin, aiding in better sleep.

In this chapter, we've explored the various forces that can disrupt the circadian rhythm, from lifestyle choices like irregular sleep patterns to the modern-day threats of blue light and chronic stress. The impact of these disruptions on our physical, mental, and emotional well-being is profound, as they interfere with our body's natural cycles, leading to consequences that stretch beyond just feeling tired. However, recognizing the problem is just the first step. As we move forward into the next chapter, we will dive into how these disruptions actively break the rhythm, further unraveling our biological clock. Understanding how the rhythm can be broken is crucial before we can explore the solutions to restore harmony in the chapters that follow. By acknowledging the complexities of what disrupts our circadian rhythm, we are now ready to turn our attention to the process of breaking it—and, ultimately, how we can take action to stop this cascade and regain control over our health.

# Breaking the rhythm

It starts out quietly. A cup of coffee at an hour you vowed not to have, a late-night binge-watch session, or a missed morning alarm. Distractions abound in modern life, each note pulling us more away from our innate rhythm. However, the most significant interruptions frequently go unreported because they are passed off as modern conveniences like technology, erratic schedules, and relentless demands. Disrupting the circadian rhythm is a consequence of adaptation rather than an act of rebellion. But at what cost?

Earlier, we went over how the human body uses the circadian rhythm, an antiquated timekeeping mechanism. Under the control of brain's suprachiasmatic nucleus (SCN), this system regulates sleep, energy, appetite, and even mood in accordance with the Earth's 24-hour cycle. It's an intricate system that guarantees that our body works in harmony. However, it's precision hinges on consistency, this fragile balance is often destroyed by modern life. although we've touched on the fundamentals of this rhythm.. it's crucial to understand how effortlessly it can loose falter in the modern world and in this chapter, we'll explore just that!

Starting with one we're all victims to, Artificial light. It stretches the day beyond natural limits, screens emit blue wavelengths that fool our brains into thinking daylight persists, and a global workforce demands activity at all hours. Each of these disruptions erodes the natural harmony of our circadian rhythm, leaving our internal clocks struggling to stay in sync with the world around us, the IRL world!

The advent of artificial lighting revolutionized human life, but did it sabotage on us as a angel in disguise ? Before the electric bulb, people lived by the rhythm of the sun—rising with the dawn and settling with dusk. Today, artificial lights extend our waking hours well into the night, interfering with melatonin production, the hormone that governs our sleep-wake cycle. More insidiously, the blue light emitted by screens tricks the body into thinking it's still daytime. This delays melatonin production which makes it harder to fall asleep, ultimately degrading the quality of rest one gets. And what drives this force of this disruption you ask? it's the angel in disguise! it's the Technology. Smartphones, laptops, and televisions have evolved into extensions of our being, constantly pulling us into the digital world even after night falls. Social media algorithms operate 24/7, and the glow of screens clashes with the natural light-dark cycle that has governed human existence for millennia. On youth, the impact is even more pronounced. Notifications, endless scrolling, and the underlying fear of missing out (FOMO) keep the mind agitated and engaged when it should be preparing for rest.

The world no longer sleeps. Night shifts, 24-hour customer service, and the pressure to be constantly productive leave little room for rest. For youth, this is especially cruel. The teenage brain is already wired for late nights and late mornings—a phase known as the delayed sleep phase syndrome (DSPS). Combine this with academic pressures and social obligations, and you're ready to check out with a recipe for perpetual jet lag that is a gene mutation which disrupts sleep almost like a jet lag but without travel.

The consequences of such practices go far beyond fatigue. Chronic circadian disruption has been linked to serious health conditions including,

**Obesity**: Irregular eating patterns affect metabolism, leading to weight gain.
**Diabetes**: Insulin sensitivity decreases when the circadian rhythm is misaligned.
**Heart Disease**: Increased stress and poor sleep quality put a strain on cardiovascular health.
**Mental Health Disorders**: Anxiety, depression, and mood swings are closely tied to disrupted rhythms.
**Premature Aging**: Cellular repair processes are hindered, accelerating aging.
**PCOS and Hormonal Disorders**: Conditions like Polycystic Ovary Syndrome are exacerbated by circadian disruption, with symptoms such as irregular periods, weight gain, and insulin resistance becoming more pronounced.

At the price of our health, some disturbances have been normalised in today's society, sometimes even glorified. Consider "grind culture," which glorifies sleepless nights as a sign of productivity. Or the acceptance of missing breakfast due to hurried mornings. Every one of these "modern habits" erodes the core of our well-being.

**Skipping Meals**: Irregular eating patterns disrupt metabolic processes, often resulting in energy crashes and weight gain. Skipping meals, especially breakfast, forces the body into a stress response, elevating cortisol levels and causing long-term damage. Some people turn to coffee as a substitute for meals, believing it can suppress appetite and aid in weight loss. While coffee may temporarily curb hunger, it doesn't provide the necessary nutrients the body needs to function, and over time, this reliance only exacerbates metabolic imbalances, contributing to more stress and disruption.

**Caffeine as a Crutch**: Over-relying on coffee to stave off fatigue masks underlying exhaustion, creating a dangerous cycle of dependency. While it may offer a temporary burst of energy, caffeine ultimately disrupts natural rhythms, leading to adrenal fatigue, heightened anxiety, and poor sleep quality. This constant need for stimulation only perpetuates the stress on our systems.

**Social Jet Lag:** Irregular sleep patterns, especially staying up late on weekends and trying to catch up during the week, confound the body's internal clock, resulting in a form of social jet lag. This disoriented state mimics the effects of jet lag without the travel, further complicating the struggle to maintain balance in our rhythms.

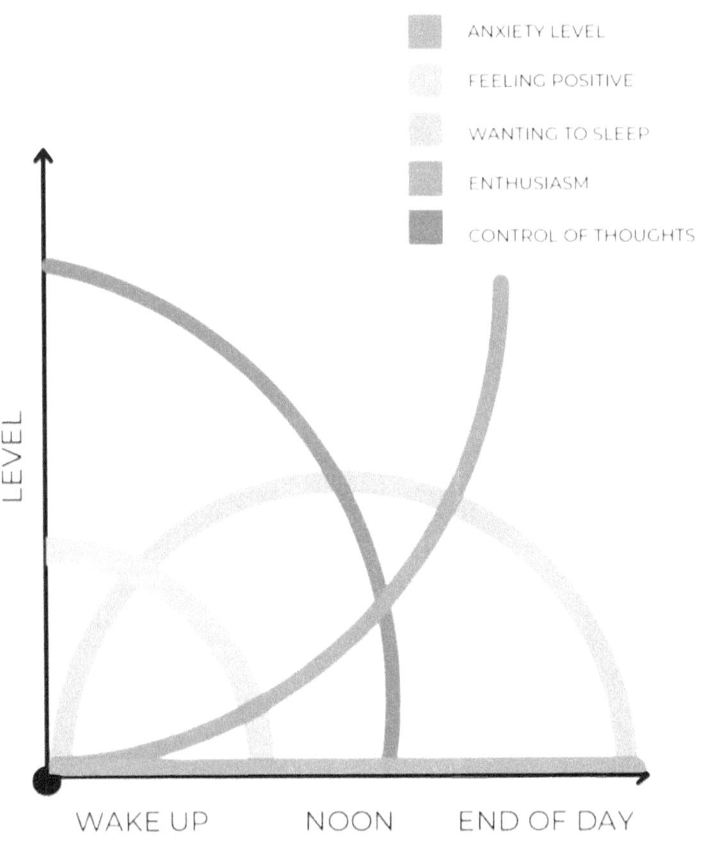
The day after a
BAD NIGHT OF SLEEP
ANXIETY LEVEL
FEELING POSITIVE
WANTING TO SLEEP
ENTHUSIASM
CONTROL OF THOUGHTS
LEVEL
WAKE UP
NOON
END OF DAY

# Reconnecting with your rhythm

Reconnecting with your circadian rhythm isn't about making drastic changes all at once. Instead, it's actually about gradually realigning your daily habits to support your body's natural cycles. Small, intentional adjustments can have a powerful impact on your overall well-being. This chapter serves as a practical guide, giving you clear steps you can take in your daily activities, sleep, meals, and study routines, all supported by evidence-based practices to help you regain balance.

Establish positive morning and night routines

Do not drink too much caffeine or alcohol

Connect to the earth - walk barefoot in grass or sand

Eat a balanced and nourishing diet

Avoid too much screen time

Gentle stretching or yoga before bed

Improve sleep hygiene

Go to bed an hour earlier

## 1. <u>Optimize Your Sleep Schedule</u>

Sleep is the cornerstone of your circadian rhythm. The first step in realigning your body is to create a sleep schedule that works with your natural cycle.

**Action Steps:**

- **Set a Consistent Bedtime and Wake Time:** Aim to wake up and go to sleep at the same time every day. Yes, even on weekends! This helps reset your internal clock and stabilizes your rhythm. Try to keep your wake-up time and bedtime within a 30-minute window each day. You might notice that it takes a week or two for your body to fully adjust, but once it does, you'll feel more refreshed and alert in the morning.

*Tip: Use an alarm on your phone or a reminder on your calendar to ensure you stick to this schedule. And, if you're tempted to stay up late, try setting an evening reminder to signal the wind-down time!*

- **Wind Down Before Bed:** Create a ritual that signals to your body that it's time to rest. This could mean reading a book, meditating, or taking a warm bath. Give yourself at least 30 minutes of screen-free time before bed—no phones, tablets, or computers. The blue light from screens interferes with melatonin production (that hormone responsible for sleep). Try incorporating something soothing, like dim lighting, to gently transition your mind into relaxation mode.

*Try This: When you put your phone away, switch to a candle or soft lighting to help your body release the melatonin it needs.*

- **Avoid Napping Late in the Day:** If you feel the need for a nap, try to keep it earlier in the day (before 3 PM). Napping too late can mess with your night's sleep, making it harder to fall asleep when you want to. If you nap in the late afternoon or evening, you'll probably find yourself tossing and turning at bedtime!

## 2. <u>Align Your Daily Activities</u>

Your circadian rhythm is more than just about sleep. Your activities throughout the day, especially those in the morning and evening, play a big role in resetting your body's internal clock.

**Action Steps:**

- **Get Morning Sunlight:** Expose yourself to natural sunlight within 30 minutes of waking up. It helps reset your circadian rhythm and boosts your mood. Try to get 20-30 minutes of sunlight, whether that's stepping outside or sitting by a window. Morning sunlight helps tell your body that it's time to be awake and alert.

*Quick Tip: Even on cloudy days, try to get sunlight for a few minutes—it's still effective!*

- **Limit Artificial Light in the Evening:** As night falls, your body starts producing melatonin, signaling it's time to wind down. To avoid confusing your body, try to reduce your exposure to artificial light—especially blue light from screens. Dim your lights, or, if possible, switch to warm-toned lights in the evening. This can have a positive effect on your sleep quality.

*Try This: Invest in a pair of blue light-blocking glasses or use a blue light filter on your phone or computer to block the disruptive light in the evening.*

- **Exercise at the Right Time:** Exercising during the day can help stabilize your rhythm and improve your sleep. However, working out too close to bedtime can raise your heart rate and make it difficult to wind down. Try to schedule your workouts for the morning or afternoon. If you like to exercise in the evening, opt for lighter activities like yoga or a walk instead of intense cardio.

*Quick Tip: If your morning is too rushed for exercise, try squeezing in a quick workout after school or work, it's a great way to de-stress!*

## <u>3. Adjust Your Meal Timing</u>

What you eat and when you eat can significantly impact your circadian rhythm. Food is fuel, but timing also matters.

## Action Steps:

- **Eat Larger Meals Earlier:** Your body's digestion slows down in the evening as it prepares for rest. Aim to have your heaviest meals earlier in the day (breakfast and lunch). Eating large meals late at night can cause indigestion or disrupt your sleep quality. Try to finish eating at least 2-3 hours before bedtime.

*Try This: Have a hearty breakfast or lunch, and keep dinner light. Consider a bowl of soup or a light salad to avoid feeling overly full before bed.*

- **Avoid Stimulants and Heavy Meals in the Evening:** Caffeine and heavy foods late in the day can mess with your sleep. Try to avoid caffeine after 2 PM and skip heavy or rich foods that might upset your stomach. Instead, opt for light snacks like fruit or yogurt if you're hungry before bed.

*Pro Tip: If you're sensitive to caffeine, check for hidden sources like chocolate or soda that can disrupt your sleep too.*

- **Hydrate Properly:** Staying hydrated is important, but too much water close to bedtime can cause you to wake up to use the bathroom. Try drinking enough water during the day so you don't need a lot right before bed.

*Try This: Make a habit of drinking water throughout the day. A good rule of thumb is to aim for 8 cups of water, or more if you're active!*

## 4. <u>Fine-Tune Your Study and Work Time</u>

When it comes to productivity, understanding your natural rhythm can help you work smarter, not harder.

**Action Steps:**
- **Work When You're Most Alert:** Everyone has a time of day when they're naturally more focused. For some, it's in the morning, and for others, it's in the late afternoon. Pay attention to your energy levels and tackle more challenging tasks during your peak focus times. You might find that your productivity skyrockets when you work during these natural energy surges.

*Quick Tip: Start your day with your most demanding tasks and leave easier ones for later in the day, that's when you'll feel more drained.*

- **Use the Pomodoro Technique:** The Pomodoro technique is a simple way to maintain focus while preventing burnout. Work in focused blocks of time (25 minutes), followed by a 5-minute break. After four blocks, take a longer break of 15-30 minutes. This rhythm of working and resting can help improve focus and productivity without draining your energy.

*Try This: Use a timer or Pomodoro app to help you stay on track. Set a goal for how many "Pomodoros" you want to complete each day.*

- **Avoid Late-Night Study Sessions:** It's tempting to study late into the night, but the brain doesn't function as well in the late hours. Try to finish your study or work at least an hour before your designated bedtime. This gives your brain time to unwind and prepare for rest. And if your reason for staying back late at night is because "i just don't have enough time!" then going bed at time and starting your day early will give you a kickstart and you'll have enough time. while adapting to this could take time but in a week of doing so you'll observe change!

*Fact: There isn't anything such as being a NIGHT OWL ! IT'S ALL IN YOUR HEAD.*

## 5. <u>Deem The Diet</u>

What you eat can significantly impact your circadian rhythm. Your body's internal clock is highly responsive to the timing and types of food you consume, and what you eat can either support or disrupt your natural cycles.

## Action Steps:

- **Eat Balanced Meals at the Right Times:** Your body is naturally attuned to certain eating patterns. Try to structure your meals to align with your circadian rhythm. Aim for a larger, nutrient-dense breakfast, followed by a moderate lunch, and a lighter dinner. This meal timing helps your digestive system process food more efficiently during the day when your body is most active.

*Quick Tip: A hearty breakfast (rich in protein and healthy fats) will provide long-lasting energy and help stabilize your blood sugar levels throughout the day.*

- **Incorporate Circadian-Friendly Foods:** Certain foods can enhance your body's natural rhythm. For example, foods rich in magnesium (like leafy greens, nuts, and seeds) can help relax your body and prepare you for sleep. Likewise, try incorporating foods with a high tryptophan content (such as turkey, eggs, and dairy) to promote melatonin production in the evening.

*Try This: Snack on a handful of almonds or pumpkin seeds in the evening to help support your sleep without disrupting your routine.*

- **Limit Caffeine and Sugary Foods:** Consuming caffeine too late in the day can interfere with your ability to fall asleep. Avoid caffeinated beverages after 2 PM. Similarly, sugar spikes can mess with your energy levels, leaving you feeling sluggish or wired at the wrong times. If you're craving something sweet, opt for a piece of fruit instead of a sugary treat.

*Quick Tip: If you have a sweet tooth, try a warm chamomile tea before bed, it's calming and naturally caffeine-free.*

- **Hydrate Wisely:** Hydration plays a crucial role in balancing your circadian rhythm. Drink plenty of water throughout the day, but avoid drinking too much right before bed to prevent sleep disruptions. Opt for herbal teas in the evening to keep hydration levels up without the risk of waking up to use the bathroom.

*Try This: Keep a water bottle with you throughout the day to ensure you're consistently hydrated. A good goal is 8 cups of water, but this may vary depending on your activity level.*

# The benefits of stying in sync

In the constant chaos of modern life, staying in sync with our circadian rhythm can feel like an impossible task. Yet, the rewards of realignment are vast and transformative. When we honor the ancient timekeeping mechanism within us, we don't just survive—we thrive. This chapter explores the profound benefits of living in harmony with our natural rhythms, revealing how it can uplift our mental health, supercharge productivity, and fortify physical well-being.

## 1. Mental Health: A Fountain of Calm and Clarity

Imagine waking up not groggy but refreshed, your mind sharp, your thoughts clear. This isn't a fantasy—it's the reward of living in sync with your body's clock. The circadian rhythm regulates the brain's production of key hormones like serotonin, the happiness hormone, and cortisol, the stress manager. When this rhythm is intact, your mood stabilizes, anxiety recedes, and a profound sense of calm takes root.

The benefits are tangible:

- Improved emotional stability: Those who maintain regular sleep cycles experience fewer mood swings.
- Enhanced focus and memory: The brain processes and stores memories during deep sleep, ensuring that you wake up with mental clarity.
- Reduced risk of mental health disorders: Studies link circadian misalignment to depression, anxiety, and even conditions like bipolar disorder.

Living in sync with your rhythm isn't just self-care, it's a lifeline for your mental well-being.

## 2. Productivity: Supercharging Your Potential

Are you tired of feeling busy but unproductive? The secret lies in leveraging your natural energy peaks and valleys. The circadian rhythm governs your body's cycles of alertness, ensuring that you're primed for focus at some times of the day and ready for rest at others.

Morning Magic: Your brain thrives on morning sunlight, which triggers the release of cortisol, providing energy for deep focus and strategic tasks.

Afternoon Groove: Use this time for teamwork or lighter tasks as your energy slightly dips.

Evening Creativity: As the day winds down, your mind is naturally inclined toward reflection, journaling, and creative pursuits.

Working with your body rather than against it eliminates the burnout of endless hustle. Productivity isn't about squeezing every moment dry; it's about thriving in your natural flow.

## 3. Physical Health: A Fortress of Strength and Resilience

When the circadian rhythm is aligned, your body becomes a fortress—resilient against modern-day ailments and illnesses. Every cell in your body operates on a 24-hour cycle, and disrupting this rhythm puts undue stress on your systems. But when you restore the balance, the benefits are astounding:

- Deep, Restorative Sleep: Consistency in sleep timing enhances the quality of your rest, allowing your body to repair tissues, build immunity, and reset for the day ahead.
- Metabolic Boost: Eating in sync with your body's natural meal times optimizes digestion, reducing the risk of obesity and diabetes.
- Heart Health: Circadian alignment reduces inflammation and stress, lowering the risk of cardiovascular diseases.
- Balanced Hormones: For women, aligning with natural rhythms can regulate cycles, reduce PCOS symptoms, and improve overall hormonal health.

Living in sync also makes your body more resilient to external stresses, acting as a shield against the wear and tear of modern life.

## 4. **Emotional Resilience: A Calm in the Storm**

It's easy to feel overwhelmed in a world that never seems to pause. But staying in sync gives you an anchor—a steadying force in turbulent times. Consistent sleep patterns and natural light exposure regulate mood hormones, making it easier to handle stress and maintain a positive outlook.
On a social level, the benefits are profound. Rested minds and balanced emotions lead to better communication, deeper empathy, and more fulfilling relationships. When you align with your rhythm, you're not just calmer—you're kinder, both to yourself and others.

## 5. **Longevity: Adding Life to Your Years**

What if the secret to aging gracefully wasn't found in a serum but in the rising and setting of the sun? Studies show that individuals who follow their circadian rhythm experience:

- Improved cellular repair: Deep sleep activates processes that repair DNA and combat oxidative stress.
- Reduced risk of age-related diseases: Conditions like Alzheimer's and Parkinson's are less common among those who maintain consistent sleep patterns.
- Youthful vitality: Regular rhythms support collagen production, immune health, and overall physical resilience.

Living in sync isn't just about adding years to your life—it's about ensuring those years are vibrant and full of potential.

Imagine a life where your alarm clock doesn't startle you awake but gently nudges you into the morning. Where meals are savored, not rushed, and rest is a sacred ritual, not an afterthought. Picture yourself energized, clear-headed, and thriving—not surviving.
This isn't an unreachable ideal. It's the gift of living in sync with your rhythm. And the best part? The first step is as simple as basking in the morning sunlight or going to bed at the same time each night. Let this chapter be your turning point. The rhythm is already within you, waiting to be rediscovered. Will you answer its call?

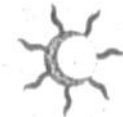

# Personalise your rhythm plan

You've learned the what and the why of the circadian rhythm. Now, it's time for the how. This chapter is your personal guide to designing a rhythm plan that fits seamlessly into your lifestyle. Think of it as building a blueprint for harmony—tailored just for you.

**Step 1: Where Are You Out of Sync?**

Before we dive into solutions, let's identify where your rhythm might be faltering. Take this quick quiz:

**Self-Assessment Quiz**

- Do you wake up and go to bed at the same time every day?
     Yes     No
- How often do you skip breakfast?
     Rarely     Sometimes     Often
- Do you consume caffeine after 3 PM?
     Yes     No
- How much time do you spend on screens before bed?
     None     1-2 hours     More than 2 hours
- How often do you eat late at night?
     Rarely     Sometimes     Often

## What Your Score Says About You

Note: Based on your responses, calculate your score by assigning 1 point for each "No," "Rarely," or "None" response, and 2 points for "Sometimes" or "1-2 hours," and 3 points for "Yes," "Often," or "More than 2 hours."

- 5–7 Misaligned Habits:

Your rhythm is in serious need of realignment. Your body is likely struggling with significant disruptions to your natural rhythm. Start by addressing the biggest offenders—late-night screen time, inconsistent meals, or inconsistent sleep. Focus on building a foundation with small, consistent changes like setting a regular bedtime. Over time, you'll see meaningful improvements in how you feel and function.

- 3–4 Misaligned Habits:

You're halfway there but could use some consistency. You're already on the right track, but a little more consistency will make a huge difference. Begin by focusing on your biggest challenges, like the times you eat, your screen habits, or your wake-up schedule. Setting clear boundaries and being more mindful of your actions will help you align more closely with your body's natural rhythms.

- 0–2 Misaligned Habits:

You're thriving, but there's always room for refinement. You're doing great! Your rhythm is strong, but you can still fine-tune your routine for even greater harmony. Consider strengthening your connection with natural light by getting more sun exposure or trying energy-boosting practices like mindful morning rituals. Small tweaks can take you from good to great.

## Step 2: Design Your Day in Sync with the Rhythm

Now that you've gathered insights from your self-assessment, it's time to create a personalized plan that integrates the key elements of a rhythm-aligned lifestyle. In this step, we'll look at everything from your morning routine and mealtimes to evening wind-down rituals. This holistic approach will help you realign your body's internal clock and enhance your overall well-being.

### Morning Routine:

- Wake-Up Time: Commit to waking up at the same time every day, even on weekends. Consistency is key in resetting your body's internal clock.

- Sunlight Exposure: Aim for at least 10-15 minutes of natural sunlight exposure within the first hour of waking. Natural light is essential for regulating your circadian rhythm and boosting your mood and energy levels.

- Hydrate and Energize: Start your day by drinking water to hydrate your body after a night of rest. Follow it up with a nutrient-dense breakfast that aligns with your body's energy needs.

- Suggested Breakfast: Opt for locally available, wholesome foods like poha with peanuts, masala oats, idli with sambar, or paratha with yogurt. These provide a balance of slow-release energy and proteins to kickstart your metabolism and keep you feeling energized throughout the morning.

**Mealtime Planner:**

A balanced, rhythm-aligned diet isn't just about timing your meals; it's about the types of foods you consume, and more importantly, choosing foods that are locally grown and aligned with your natural environment. Eating foods that your body has adapted to over generations is crucial to syncing with your circadian rhythm. Here's how you can design your meals:

- Breakfast:
    - Suggested Foods: Poha, upma, paratha with yogurt, or a smoothie with curd, fruits, and nuts.
    - Why It Works: A nutrient-rich breakfast stabilizes your blood sugar, giving you energy for the day. Foods like poha or paratha provide slow-release energy, while yogurt or nuts offer protein and healthy fats to keep you full and focused.

- Lunch:
    - Suggested Foods: Dal with rice, vegetable curry with roti, khichdi, or chickpea salad.
    - Why It Works: Lunch should be your heaviest meal, providing a good balance of protein, complex carbs, and healthy fats. Foods like dal and roti provide long-lasting energy and prevent afternoon fatigue. These meals also support muscle repair and overall metabolic function.

- Dinner:
    - Suggested Foods: Light vegetable soups, dal-chawal, grilled paneer with veggies, or a vegetable curry with quinoa or brown rice.
    - Why It Works: A light, balanced dinner allows your body to wind down for sleep without overburdening your digestive system. Focus on easily digestible meals that support cellular repair and rejuvenation during the night.

## The Importance of Eating Local Foods:

Eating local, seasonal foods not only nourishes your body but also strengthens your connection with the environment around you. Our genes have adapted to the foods that are native to our regions, so consuming locally sourced foods helps keep our circadian rhythm in tune with nature's cycles.For instance, in India, you'll find foods like lentils, rice, seasonal vegetables, and fruits that have been enjoyed for centuries for their health benefits. These foods are rich in the nutrients your body needs to perform optimally throughout the day.If you live outside of India, focus on foods native to your region that have been staples in your culture. Whether it's Mediterranean olives, East Asian rice dishes, or Western grains, these local foods are aligned with your body's natural requirements.Note: While it's exciting to try exotic or trendy diets, it's essential not to completely abandon your local food traditions. The exotic, heavily processed foods or fad diets might not support your circadian rhythm and could disrupt your digestion and metabolism. Stick to foods that your body has naturally adapted to over generations.

## Evening Wind-Down:

In the evening, your goal should be to signal your body that it's time to wind down and prepare for restful sleep. Start slowing down your activities to transition into a state of relaxation.

- Screen Cut-Off Time: Avoid screens at least 60 minutes before bedtime. Blue light from devices can disrupt melatonin production, the hormone responsible for helping you fall asleep.
- Relaxation Activity: Choose calming activities like reading a book, journaling, or engaging in light stretches or meditation. These practices signal your body that it's time to prepare for a restful night.

**Other Elements to Support a Rhythm-Aligned Lifestyle:**

- Exercise: Regular physical activity, especially during the day, is crucial for syncing your body's internal clock. Aim for 20-30 minutes of moderate exercise, such as walking, yoga, or cycling. Avoid intense workouts close to bedtime, as they can increase adrenaline and disrupt your sleep.
- Sleep Environment: Your bedroom should be a sanctuary for rest. Keep it cool, dark, and quiet to encourage deep sleep. Consider using blackout curtains, white noise machines, or sleep masks if necessary.
- Consistency is Key: The most important factor in realigning your rhythm is consistency. Stick to your plan as much as possible and avoid major disruptions like irregular sleep patterns, late-night screen use, or inconsistent meal times.

**Other Elements to Support a Rhythm-Aligned Lifestyle:**

1. Exercise: Regular physical activity, especially during the day, is crucial for syncing your body's internal clock. Aim for 20-30 minutes of moderate exercise, such as walking, yoga, or cycling. Avoid intense workouts close to bedtime, as they can increase adrenaline and disrupt your sleep.
2. Sleep Environment: Your bedroom should be a sanctuary for rest. Keep it cool, dark, and quiet to encourage deep sleep. Consider using blackout curtains, white noise machines, or sleep masks if necessary.
3. Consistency is Key: The most important factor in realigning your rhythm is consistency. Stick to your plan as much as possible and avoid major disruptions like irregular sleep patterns, late-night screen use, or inconsistent meal times.

**Personalizing Your Rhythm Plan:**

Everyone's circadian rhythm is unique, so feel free to adjust your plan as needed. If you work night shifts or have other lifestyle factors that impact your schedule, consider seeking professional advice on how to best realign your rhythm. The goal is to create a routine that supports your body's natural cycles and promotes optimal well-being.

By following this holistic approach—balancing nutritious, local foods, consistent sleep habits, and self-care routines—you will gradually notice positive changes in your energy levels, mood, and overall health.

## Step 3: Your Rhythm-Aligned Challenges

Ready to integrate your circadian rhythm into daily life? These challenges will help you take actionable steps and see real improvements. Commit to these to start aligning your routine.

*Screen-Free Nights :*

For the next 7 days, avoid all screens (phones, tablets, computers, TV) for at least an hour before bedtime.

- Challenge Goal: Track your sleep quality and morning alertness. How does the absence of screens impact your rest?

*Consistent Wake-Up Time:*

Choose a wake-up time that works for you and stick to it every day, even on weekends, for 30 days.

- Challenge Goal: Monitor your energy levels and how quickly you feel awake in the mornings. Does your body start feeling naturally alert?

*Balanced Breakfast:*

Start your day with a nutritious, balanced breakfast every day for 7 days. Ensure it includes protein and healthy fats.

- Challenge Goal: Track how your focus, energy, and mood shift throughout the morning. Does it make a noticeable difference in how you feel?

*Connecting With Nature:*

Spend at least 15 minutes outside in natural light every morning within an hour of waking for 7 days.

- Challenge Goal: Observe your mood, energy, and sleep quality at the end of each day. How does sunlight exposure impact your rhythm?

*Meal Timing :*

Commit to eating lunch no later than 2 PM for 7 days, and avoid eating past 8 PM.

- Challenge Goal: Note how this affects your digestion, energy, and sleep quality. Does eating earlier help your overall routine?

*The Evening Wind-Down Challenge:*

Create a 30-minute evening routine that helps you wind down (e.g., light reading, stretching, or meditating). Do this every evening for 7 days.

- Challenge Goal: Track how relaxed you feel before sleep and how quickly you fall asleep. Does a calm routine lead to better rest?

*The Hydration Challenge:*
Start your day by drinking a glass of water as soon as you wake up and keep a hydration goal throughout the day. Aim for at least 2 liters of water daily for 7 days.
- Challenge Goal: Monitor how hydration impacts your energy, focus, and digestion. How do you feel when you stay properly hydrated?

*The Movement Challenge:*
Incorporate at least 30 minutes of physical activity into your day, whether through walking, yoga, or light exercises. Commit to doing this daily for 7 days.
- Challenge Goal: Notice any changes in your sleep patterns and daily energy levels. How does regular movement influence your rhythm?

*The Caffeine Cutback Challenge:*
Gradually reduce caffeine intake. If you usually drink coffee after 3 PM, try cutting it off by 12 PM for a week.
- Challenge Goal: Track how this affects your sleep and energy. Does reducing caffeine help you sleep better and feel more energized in the morning?

**Track Your Progress!**
- Reflection Journaling: Keep a daily journal to note how each challenge affects your sleep, energy, and mood.
- Progress Tracker: Mark off each day you complete a challenge to stay motivated.

## Step 4: Avoid These Hidden Disruptors

Even with the best rhythm-alignment plan, small habits can sneak in and quietly disrupt your progress. These hidden disruptors may not be immediately obvious, but they have a significant impact on your body's natural cycle. Let's explore these subtle yet impactful habits that could be silently undermining your circadian rhythm.

1. Preservative-Laden Foods:
Processed and preserved foods, especially those packed with artificial additives and preservatives, can throw off your body's metabolic processes. They are often high in refined sugars, unhealthy fats, and sodium, which can spike your blood sugar, interfere with your digestion, and negatively affect your energy levels throughout the day. Tip: Opt for fresh, whole foods—fruits, vegetables, grains, and proteins—that are minimally processed. These nutrient-dense options nourish your body and align with your circadian rhythm.

2. Late-Night Snacking:
It's tempting to indulge in a late-night snack, but eating too close to bedtime disrupts your sleep cycle. Late-night meals trigger insulin production and keep your digestive system active when it should be resting, preventing your body from properly preparing for sleep. Tip: If you need a snack in the evening, choose light, easy-to-digest options like a small serving of nuts or yogurt, and try to eat at least 2–3 hours before bedtime. This will allow your body to focus on sleep, not digestion.

3. Overuse of Caffeine:
While a cup of coffee or tea may seem like the perfect pick-me-up, excessive caffeine—especially after 3 PM—can disrupt your natural sleep-wake cycle. Caffeine stimulates the production of cortisol, a hormone that keeps you alert, but too much can lead to restlessness and difficulty falling asleep at night. Tip: Limit caffeine consumption to earlier in the day, and aim to switch to herbal teas or warm water in the evening to avoid overstimulating your system.

4. Blue Light Exposure After Dark:
Most of us know that screens can keep us up at night, but the blue light emitted from phones, tablets, and computers suppresses melatonin, the hormone responsible for sleep. This can confuse your body's internal clock and make it harder to fall asleep. Tip: Use blue light filters on your devices, or better yet, avoid screens altogether an hour before bedtime. Switch to reading or listening to calming music instead to signal to your body that it's time to wind down.

5. Social Jet Lag:
Irregular sleep patterns over the weekend or during holidays can cause "social jet lag," a phenomenon where your body clock is misaligned with your routine. Skipping your regular sleep schedule during the weekend can make it harder to readjust to a healthy rhythm on Monday. Tip: Try to keep your weekend sleep schedule consistent with your weekday routine. If you need to adjust, aim for small, gradual changes rather than drastic shifts.

6. Skipping Meals or Eating Too Late:
Not eating on time can lead to an irregular metabolic pattern, affecting your energy levels throughout the day. Skipping meals, especially breakfast, can cause blood sugar spikes and dips, leading to energy crashes. Similarly, eating too late disturbs your body's natural digestion processes. Tip: Aim to eat regular, balanced meals at the same time every day. If you feel hungry late at night, opt for a small, light snack but try to avoid large meals close to bedtime.

7. Dehydration:
Dehydration is one of the most overlooked disruptors. Your body needs adequate water for metabolic and biological functions, and dehydration can lead to fatigue, poor sleep, and a weakened immune system. Tip: Drink water consistently throughout the day, but avoid large amounts right before bed to prevent waking up during the night.

8. Excessive Work or Physical Activity:
Overworking or excessive physical exertion can lead to adrenal fatigue, where your body's stress response is constantly activated, leaving you feeling tired and worn out. This can interfere with both your energy levels during the day and your ability to fall asleep at night. Tip: Balance work and physical activity with enough downtime. Incorporate rest days into your exercise routine, and give your body time to recover from the demands of daily life.

9. Inconsistent Light Exposure:
Your body depends on exposure to natural light during the day to regulate its circadian rhythm. Lack of sunlight, especially in the morning, can delay the production of melatonin in the evening. Tip: Make an effort to spend at least 10–15 minutes outside in natural light in the morning. If that's not possible, consider using a light therapy box to simulate sunlight.

Eliminating hidden disruptors and adjusting small habits can help to align with your circadian rhythm. It's not just about when you sleep, but about considering every aspect of your daily routine.

## Step 5: Reflect and Adjust

Now that you've taken the time to design and implement your rhythm plan, it's important to pause and reflect on your progress. Self-awareness is key to maintaining long-term success with your circadian alignment.

**Take a moment to consider:**
- What's one habit you can change immediately to align with your circadian rhythm?
- Think about small, achievable changes that could have a big impact. Perhaps it's cutting back on late-night screen time or adjusting your sleep schedule on weekends.
- How would your life improve if you consistently felt rested and energized?
- Consider how better sleep and energy levels would affect your daily life—your productivity, mood, and overall well-being. Imagine the benefits of a healthier, more balanced routine.

Write your answers here or in a journal.
Reflecting on these questions will help you stay motivated as you continue your journey towards aligning with your circadian rhythm. Use your answers as a source of inspiration to make adjustments along the way. Don't be afraid to tweak your plan if something isn't working—this is a continuous process of growth and self-discovery.

# Staying on track

Transitioning to a circadian rhythm-aligned lifestyle is a transformative journey. While you may feel prepared after learning the why and how, the reality of life —school deadlines, social gatherings, and digital distractions—can derail even the best plans. This chapter focuses on staying committed, overcoming obstacles, and maintaining consistency without sacrificing other aspects of your life.

Why Staying on Track Matters?
Consistency is the cornerstone of aligning with your circadian rhythm. Every disruption, from late-night cramming sessions to endless screen time, creates ripple effects, impacting your sleep, energy, and overall well-being. Staying on track isn't about perfection; it's about creating sustainable habits that withstand life's unpredictability.

## 1. Motivation in Motion: Building Momentum

Keeping your enthusiasm alive is essential. Motivation can waver, but consistency bridges the gap between inspiration and lasting change.

- Start Small, Stay Steady: Focus on one habit at a time. For instance, begin by fixing your wake-up time before tackling meal schedules or reducing screen time.
- Track Your Progress: Whether it's through a digital app or a simple journal, noting your sleep quality, energy levels, and mood can help you see the tangible benefits of your effort.
- Reward Yourself: Celebrate milestones. Did you stick to a consistent sleep schedule for a week? Treat yourself—whether it's a favorite activity or a relaxing evening.

## 2. Technology: Friend or Foe?

Digital devices are part of modern life, but they don't have to disrupt your rhythm. Learn to manage their influence effectively.

- Tech Curfews: Make the hour before bedtime a screen-free zone. Use that time to relax, read, or engage in non-digital hobbies.
- Leverage Digital Tools: Use apps that promote healthy habits. Reminders for bedtime, guided meditations, or blue-light filter apps can complement your journey.
- Focus Mode: Most smartphones have features to block notifications or limit app usage during certain hours. Set these to align with your rhythm plan.

## 3. School, Social Life, and Balance

Balancing academic demands and a social life with your circadian rhythm requires intentional planning and prioritization.

- Plan Ahead: If you know you have late-night plans, adjust your schedule to accommodate. Allow for a brief nap earlier in the day or reschedule tasks to avoid compromising sleep.
- Be Transparent: Let your friends and family know about your goals. You don't have to skip every social gathering, but communicating your needs can help them understand and support you.
- Time Management: Divide your day into focused time blocks for studying, relaxing, and socializing. Sticking to these blocks helps ensure no area dominates at the expense of your health.

## 4. Tackling Setbacks: Bounce Back Strong

Setbacks are inevitable, but how you handle them determines your success.

- Don't Dwell on Slips: A missed alarm or late-night indulgence isn't the end of the world. Reflect on what led to the slip, adjust, and move forward.
- Learn from Patterns: If you notice recurring disruptions—like staying up late for schoolwork—identify the root cause and strategize solutions, such as starting assignments earlier or seeking help.
- Resilience is Key: View challenges as opportunities to grow. Each time you overcome a hurdle, you're building habits that are more robust and adaptable.

## 5. Techniques for Consistency

Integrate these techniques into your routine to maintain alignment with your circadian rhythm:

- Morning Rituals: Start your day with intentionality. Whether it's a quick stretch, sunlight exposure, or a balanced breakfast, morning habits set the tone for the day.
- Accountability Partners: Share your journey with a friend or family member. Encouragement and shared progress make it easier to stay committed.
- Reflect and Adjust: Schedule regular check-ins with yourself. Are your routines still serving you? Life evolves, and your rhythm plan should, too.

This chapter—and this book—may be ending, but your journey is just beginning. The tools, insights, and habits you've discovered here are yours to carry forward, not as rules, but as companions in a life well-lived. Circadian rhythm alignment isn't just a lifestyle; it's a philosophy. It's a gentle yet profound reminder that our best selves emerge when we live in harmony with nature and with ourselves. So, as you close this book, ask yourself:

- What's the one habit you'll embrace first?
- How will you inspire others to find their rhythm?
- What legacy will you create by choosing balance over chaos?

The rhythm of life will always shift, but with the lessons you've learned, you have the power to adapt, align, and thrive. Stay curious, stay resilient, and most importantly, stay on track—because the best version of you is waiting to unfold.

9 7 9 8 8 9 6 9 9 1 7 7 9